CW00840359

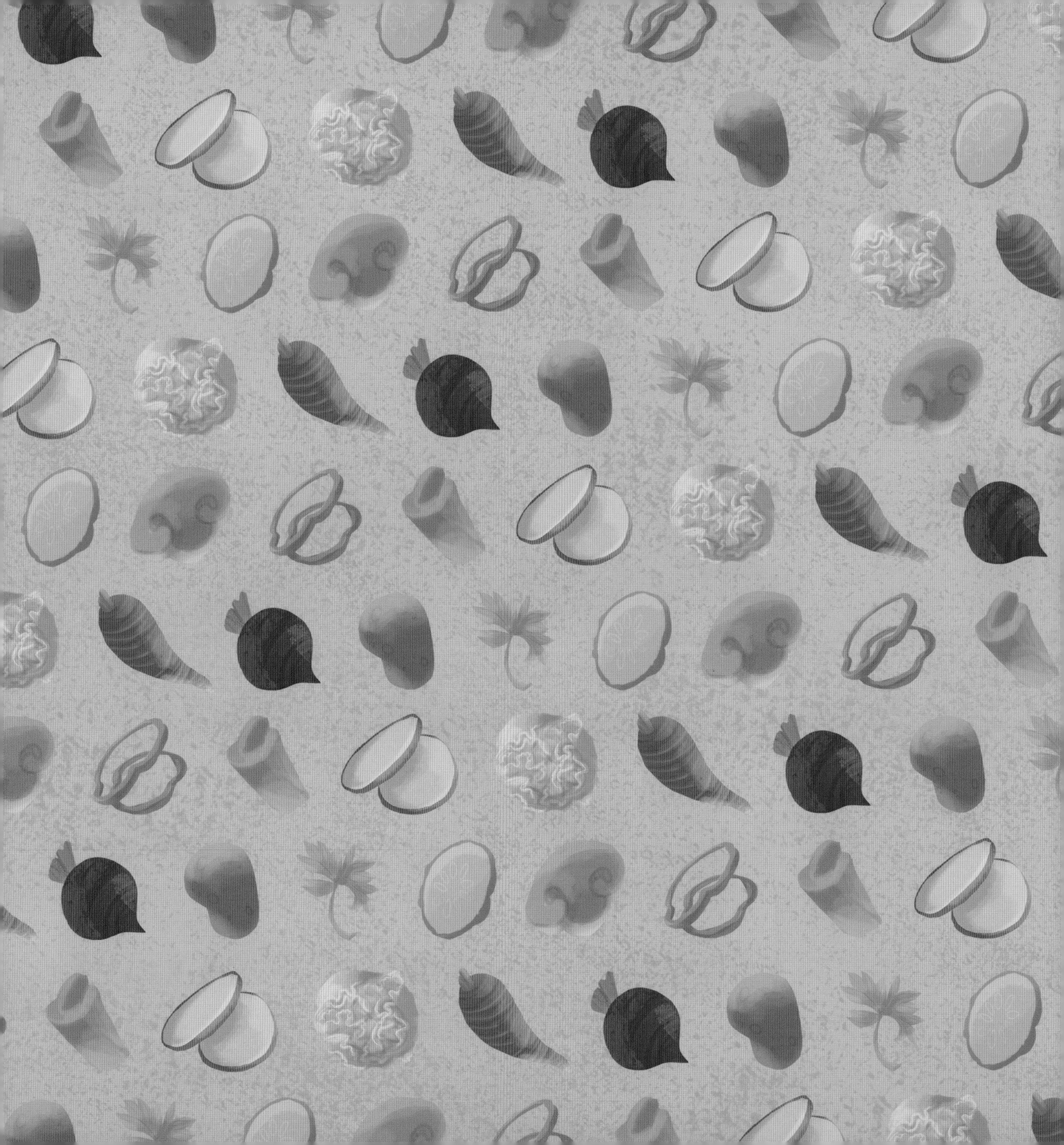

Licensed exclusively to Imagine That Publishing Ltd
Tide Mill Way, Woodbridge, Suffolk, IP12 1AP, UK
www.imaginethat.com

0 2 4 6 8 9 7 5 3 1
Manufactured in China

Written by Oakley Graham
Illustrated by Erika Meza

ISBN 978-1-78958-200-0

A catalogue record for this book is available from the British Library

Carrot Soup

a rabbity tale

Written by Oakley Graham

Illustrated by Erika Meza

Once upon a time, there was a great famine in the burrows and the rabbits jealously guarded whatever food they could find, hiding it from their best friends and neighbours.

One day, an old rabbit came to the burrows and started asking questions as if he was planning to stay. 'There's nothing to eat here,' he was told. 'You had better hop along.'

'Don't worry, I have everything I need,' said the old rabbit, smiling. 'In fact, I was thinking of making some carrot soup to share with everyone.'

The old rabbit pulled a large pot from his backpack, filled it with water, and lit a fire under it. Then, very carefully, he pulled a tiny, thin carrot from his pocket and dropped it into the water.

News of the old rabbit's offer to share his carrot soup spread fast, and before long, most of the rabbits were watching curiously from a distance.

As the old rabbit sniffed the soup and licked his lips, hunger began to overcome the other rabbits' mistrust.

'Yummy,' the old rabbit said to himself rather loudly. 'I do like a tasty carrot soup. But, carrot soup with cabbage – that really is the most wonderful rabbity treat!'

Soon a young rabbit appeared. She was holding a cabbage she'd been hiding and she shyly added it to the pot.

'Excellent!' cried the old rabbit. 'You know, I once had carrot soup with cabbage and a bit of broccoli, and it was the best soup that I have ever tasted!'

Another rabbit nervously appeared from his burrow and popped a large piece of broccoli into the pot.

And so it continued, with the old rabbit suggesting more and more ways that his carrot soup could be made even tastier.

Rabbits from all over the burrows
appeared with leafy greens ...

... parsley ...

... cucumber ...

... celery ...

... radishes ...

... peppers ...

... and mushrooms, that were all happily thrown into the pot.

For the first time in a very long time, the rabbits were laughing, smiling and working together with their friends and neighbours.

Soon the air was filled with the smell of the most delicious, most yummy, most magnificent soup the rabbits had ever seen.

That evening, every buck, doe and kitten in the burrows feasted until they could eat no more.

The next morning the old rabbit was gone and some of the cleverer rabbits realised they had been tricked!

But they also realised that the old rabbit had taught them a very important lesson.

The rabbits now work together and share, especially when it comes to making *yummy* carrot soup!

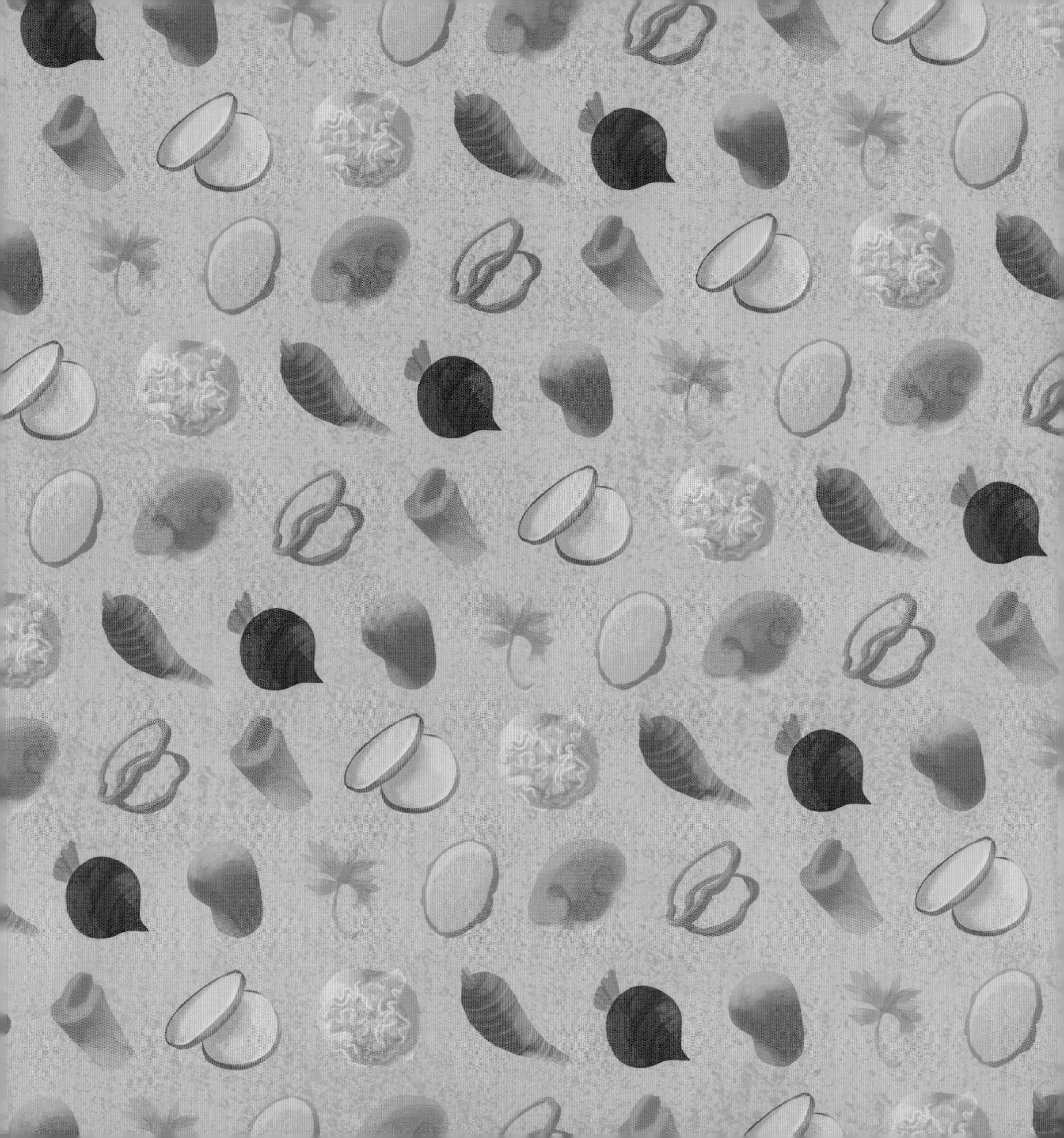

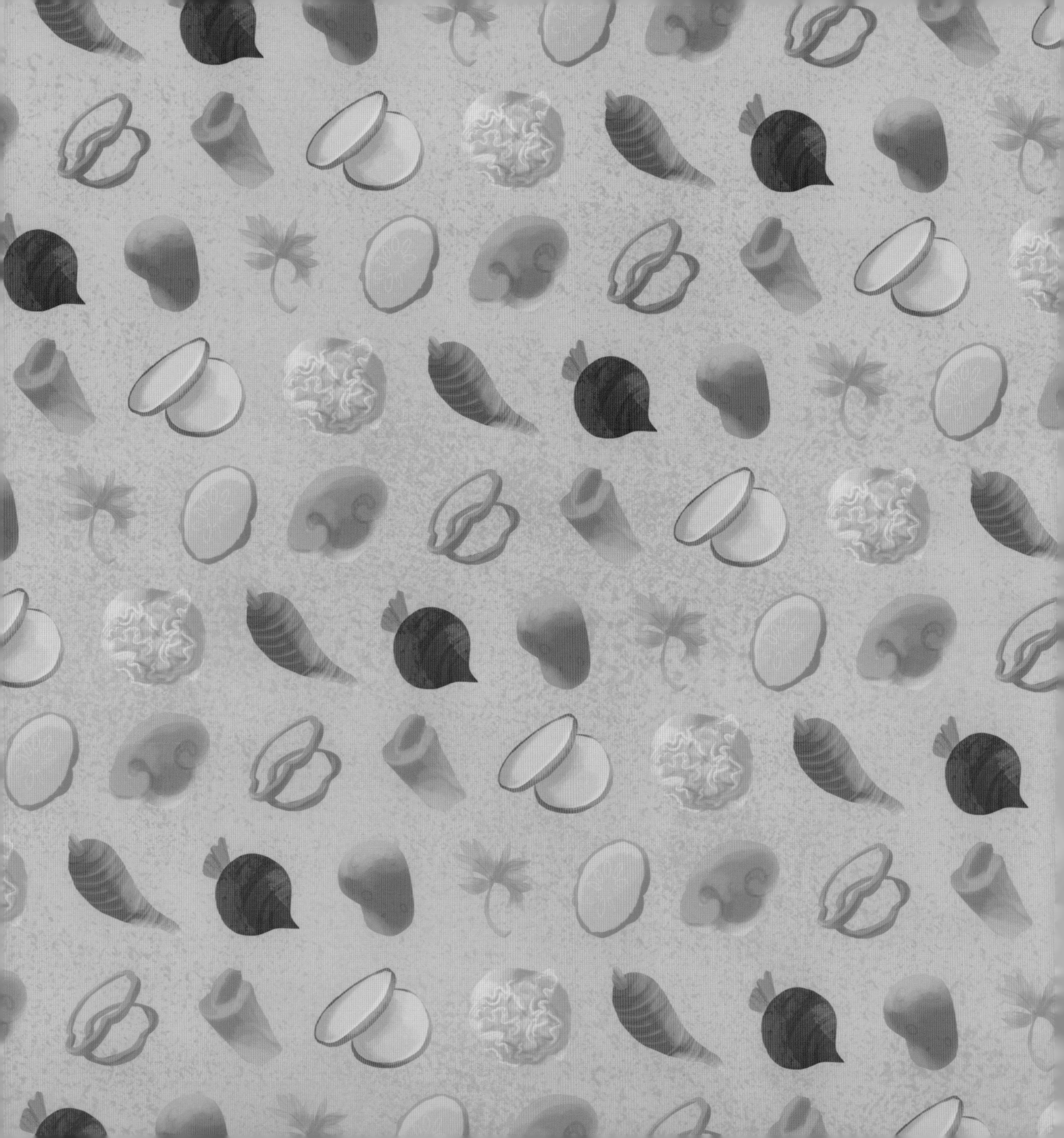